# Alligator raggedy-mouth

## Making music with poems and rhymes

**Maureen Hanke & Jacalyn Leedham**

**A & C Black · London**

First published 1996
Reprinted 2000
A & C Black (Publishers) Ltd
35 Bedford Row  London  WC1R 4JH
© 1996 A & C Black (Publishers) Ltd

ISBN 0-7136-4281-5

Poetry selected by Jacalyn Leedham
Teachers' notes by Maureen Hanke
Text © 1996 A & C Black
Cover artwork by Dee Shulman
Line drawings by Dee Shulman
Edited by Ana Sanderson
Designed by Dorothy Moir
Printed by Caligraving Ltd

# Contents

## 1 - Making up patterns of sounds

*(Simple improvisations using body sounds and untuned percussion)*

# About this book

Alligator raggedy-mouth is full of ideas for teachers of 7 - 11 year olds to encourage creative music-making in the classroom. There is a wealth of musical activities, all using poetry as the starting point. If you are a generalist teacher, you can use this book as no music reading is required and it will enable you to increase your musical confidence through your knowledge of poetry. If you are a music specialist, this book gives you the opportunity to broaden and enrich your music teaching.

## Why poetry as a starting point for music-making?

Poetry and music are two of our oldest art forms. Both involve composing, performing, listening and appraising. Both are concerned with mood, atmosphere and emotion. And both share some common vocabulary, for example, words such as structure, rhythm and phrases, though for some words, the emphasis of meaning is slightly different.

Every poem included in this collection has a special quality or feature that makes it an exciting starting point for creative music-making. If you wish to use this book for cross-curricular purposes, there is plenty more to explore in each poem than we have limited ourselves to in this book.

## Creative music-making - composing and improvising

We improvise and compose with words everyday: we improvise sentences conveying our thoughts in conversation and we compose sentences that might be read or repeated for letters, speeches, stories, poems or plays, often committing them to paper. A musical improvisation is created simultaneously with the performer thinking of musical ideas. Improvisations are not written down and no two improvisations sound the same. However, a musical composition is memorised or written down so that it can be repeated. Each performance of a composition sounds the same, though there may be some subtle differences.

Inventing music as you play it and inventing a piece of music that can be played again are both important musical skills. Yet they are also two of the hardest to teach. The aim of this book is to give you, the teacher, some starting points and activities to do which will provide your pupils with the inspiration to make music and structures within which to work.

## How the book is organised

The poems and activities have been organised into four sections broadly ranging from easy to difficult. You can either work through the book systematically or dip into it. The early material can be done successfully with 7 - 11 year olds. However, you will probably find that the material nearer the end of the book will be more suitable for 10 - 11 year olds.

Simple activities using patterns of sounds and short improvisations can be found in the first section entitled 'Making up patterns of sounds'. The second section, 'Exploring shape and structure', contains longer improvisations and suggests ways of developing and structuring ideas. The third section, 'Accompanying words with sounds', focuses on composing accompaniments for poems, while the fourth section, 'Capturing mood and atmosphere', concentrates on the children's own compositions.

## Music national curricula

The music activities that follow each poem are relevant to the performing and composing strands of the music curricula for 7-11 year olds of England, Scotland and Wales. Learning is achieved in all the musical elements: pitch, duration, texture, dynamics, timbre, tempo and musical structure.

At the end of the activities with each poem, there are descriptions of the musical skills and knowledge that the pupils will have had the opportunity to develop to some degree. These points are intended to help you assess how your pupils are progressing in their music-making.

## Classroom management

With each activity, there is a suggested grouping for the children, such as 'whole class', 'small group' or 'in pairs'.

For some of the 'whole class' activities, it is helpful if the children sit in a circle. If you do not have space for everyone to sit in a circle, you can adapt to your surroundings to do the activity. Just ensure that the children have a pre-decided order or sequence in which to perform, and that they have eye contact with you and each other.

Limit the amount of time your pupils have to work on activities, so that the children focus on the task rather than work aimlessly. When the children are working on activities in small groups or pairs, they may need suggestions to help them get started. Before dividing into groups, discuss the activity with the whole class so that the children know what they should do and have a few ideas to start them off.

## Classroom sound resources

The activities in this book require the children to use vocal sounds, body percussion sounds, untuned percussion instruments and tuned percussion instruments, (see page 6). For many of the activities, you do not need an instrument per child - indeed, it is better to have a few resources that are of a high quality than many resources that are battered, out of tune, and de-motivating. Try to build a collection of instruments that reflect world music, that include high and low pitched sounds, that are played using a range of different movements, for example, instruments you shake, hit, scrape, play with a beater, and so on. Most importantly, collect instruments that everyone can take pleasure and pride in owning.

## Preparing to enjoy the book

Once you have chosen a poem, familiarise yourself with it. Spend some preparation time reading the activities and prepare carefully for your role in them. Be clear in your mind how you will arrange the class and be ready for moments that require general movement. Decide in advance which instruments you will use, and have them out ready for you to give out or for the children to access under your instruction.

When the children make music, they should also evaluate their musical ideas. There are no right or wrong musical ideas, so both you and your pupils must trust your own ears when assessing a musical idea. Monitor your pupils progress - and be prepared for exciting results!

# Classroom sound resources

## Vocal sounds

These are sounds made by the mouth.

## Body percussion sounds

These sounds are made using the body.

## Untuned percussion instruments

This covers a wide range of instruments from all over the world, made of various different materials that can be tapped, shaken or scraped.

## Tuned percussion instruments

These instruments can play notes tuned to specific pitches.

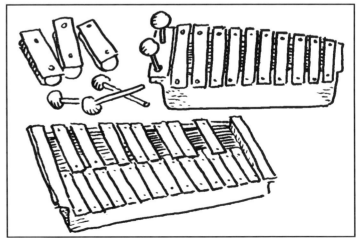

# Cats

Cats sleep
Anywhere,
Any table,
Any chair,
Top of piano,
Window ledge,
In the middle,
On the edge,
Open drawer,
Empty shoe,
Anybody's
Lap will do,
Fitted in a
Cardboard box,
In the cupboard
With your frocks -
Anywhere!
They don't care!
Cats sleep
Anywhere.

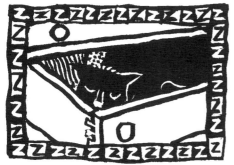

*Eleanor Farjeon*

# Cats

This poem is about various places where cats might sleep. Read it with a steady beat throughout; notice how the syllables of the words fit around the beat.

In the musical development activity, each child makes up a rhythm to clap.

## Stage 1 - introducing the poem

*(A whole class activity)*

1.  Before reading the poem to the children, have a general discussion about cats. Consider different kinds of cats, their sleeping habits, nature and appearance.

2.  Read the poem, keeping a steady beat throughout. Then ask the children to clap or tap the beat as you read. The cat heads below show the beat in the poem.

Cats    sleep    A - ny - where

A - ny    ta - ble    A - ny    chair

3.  The poem mentions several places where cats sleep. Ask the children to name as many as they can remember.

## Stage 2 - a spoken improvisation

*(A small group activity)*

In this activity, the class makes up its own version of this poem by thinking of other places where cats might sleep.

1.  All the children memorise the first two lines of the poem:

Cats    sleep    A - ny - where

2.  Divide the children into small groups of five or six. Each group thinks of one or two places where cats might sleep to make two new lines for the poem.

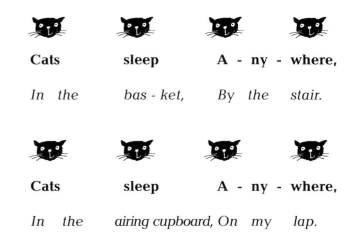

Cats    sleep    A - ny - where,

*In    the    bas - ket,    By    the    stair.*

Cats    sleep    A - ny - where,

*In    the    airing cupboard, On  my    lap.*

The words of each new pair of lines must fit around the steady beat of the poem.

In the last example 'In the airing cupboard, On my lap', the words 'airing cupboard' are said very quickly in order to fit into the steady beat. The rhythm of this line is different from the rhythms of the lines of the poem.

3.    The whole class performs its version of the poem. Everyone chants the first two lines of the poem. Then one of the small group chants its two new lines. Everyone chants the two first lines again and this is followed by another small group's new lines.

| | |
|---|---|
| *All:* | **Cats sleep** |
| | **Anywhere,** |
| *Group 1:* | *In the bedroom,* |
| | *On my bed.* |
| *All:* | **Cats sleep** |
| | **Anywhere,** |
| *Group 2:* | *In the bathtub,* |
| | *By the loo ... etc* |

Keep the beat going throughout, without pausing between lines.

## Stage 3 - a rhythmic improvisation game

*(A whole class activity)*

This activity is similar to the 'spoken improvisation' in stage 2. However, instead of making up words, the children make up rhythms to clap. (This activity can work successfully if the children either make up rhythms lasting for four beats, or longer or shorter rhythms that end clearly.)

1.    Everyone begins by clapping the rhythm of the words of the first two lines of the poem.

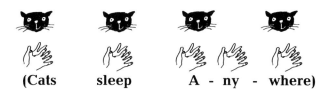

**(Cats    sleep    A - ny - where)**

2.    Then one child makes up a different rhythm to clap. The rhythm can be that of the words he or she invented with the small group; alternatively, it can be a rhythm not based on a line from the poem. Here are some example rhythms:

*(In    the    bas - ket,    By    the    stair)*

*(In    the    airing cupboard, On    my    lap)*

3.    When the child has finished clapping his or her rhythm, everyone claps the rhythm of the first two lines of the poem again. Then the next child in the circle claps a new rhythm. This process is continued until everyone has contributed a solo rhythm.

Encourage the children to think of interesting solo rhythms to clap that are different from the rhythm of the first two lines of the poem. Keep the beat going throughout.

**Musical skills and knowledge developed:**
- **Composing:** inventing rhythmic patterns and placing them correctly in a structure
- **Duration:** long and short sounds making rhythmic patterns; steady beat
- **Structure:** recurring and contrasting ideas

# Talk war

Talk war
War love
Love touch
Touch peace
Peace beat
Beat slip
Slip waste
Waste hate
Hate take
Take slice
Slice break
Break limbs
Limbs play
Play pain
Pain joy
Joy caress
Caress ploy
Ploy plan
Plan flight
Flight light

Light middle
Middle hand
Hand wave
Wave ocean
Ocean land
Land walk
Walk destroy
Destroy war
War talk
Talk stop
Stop learn
Learn to
To breathe
Breathe love
Love touch
Touch peace
Peace.

*Albie Olivierre*

# Talk war

In 'Talk war', the last word of each line is used as the first word of the next line. Because of the way the lines link with each other, we have called it a 'chain poem'. ('Seashore' on page 28 follows the same pattern.)

In the musical development activities, the children make up chains of sounds.

## Stage 1 - introducing and making up 'chain poems'

*(A whole class activity)*

The children learn about the structure of the 'chain poem' and make one up.

1. Read the poem to the class. Ask the children what they noticed about the words of the poem.

2. Explore the 'chain' structure of the poem with the class by considering in more detail a short section of four lines. Read them, pausing after each line.

> **Hand wave**
> **Wave ocean**
> **Ocean land**
> **Land walk**

Ask the children what they notice about the lines. Did anyone notice that each line consisted of only two words? Did anyone notice that the last word of each line was the first word of the next line?

3. When the children are familiar with the 'chain' structure, organise them into a circle to make up a class 'chain poem'. Each child will contribute one line to the poem. Like 'Talk war', each line should be made up of two words which should be associated with each other in some way.

4. One child thinks of two words for the first line of the poem. He or she begins the improvisation by saying them out loud. The next child in the circle thinks of the next line of the poem. He or she must use the last word of the previous line.

This process is continued until everyone in the class has contributed a line. The end result is a 'chain poem' made up by the whole class.

## Stage 2 - making up a 'sound chain'

*(A whole class activity)*

To make a 'sound chain' the class perform a series of sounds following the structure of the 'chain poem'. You can decide whether the 'sound chain' should be performed with a steady beat or freely.

If possible, the class should sit in a circle.

1. One child thinks of two different body percussion or vocal sounds to perform.

2. The next child in the circle makes two different body percussion sounds. However, the first sound must be the same as the last sound made by the previous child.

3. This pattern is continued. When everyone has performed two sounds, the 'sound chain' is complete.

## Stage 3 - more 'sound chains' with musical rules

*(A whole class activity)*

This activity develops the stage 2 activity of making up 'sound chains' by introducing musical rules about the sounds the children perform. Again, the children should sit in a circle if possible.

1. Tell the children that each pair of sounds they make must follow this rule: if the first sound is a long sound, it must be followed by a short sound; if the first sound is a short sound, it must be followed by a long sound.

If this rule is followed, there will be a pattern of sounds:

| | |
|---|---|
| *1st child:* | **long sound, short sound** |
| *2nd child:* | **short sound, long sound** |
| *3rd child:* | **long sound, short sound** |
| *4th child:* | **short sound, long sound...** |

(This pattern is easier to perform freely, rather than with a steady beat.)

2. Try a different rule for a new 'sound chain': a loud sound must be followed by a quiet sound and a quiet sound must be followed by a loud sound.

If this rule is followed, there will be a pattern of sounds:

| | |
|---|---|
| *1st child:* | **loud sound, quiet sound** |
| *2nd child:* | **quiet sound, loud sound** |
| *3rd child:* | **loud sound, quiet sound** |
| *4th child:* | **quiet sound, loud sound...** |

(This pattern can be performed freely or with a steady beat, though the latter is more difficult.)

**Musical skills and knowledge developed:**
- **Composing:** making up a sequence of sounds
- **Timbre:** different sound qualities made using the body
- **Duration:** long and short sounds
- **Dynamics:** loud and quiet sounds

# You're late

'You're late', she said.
'Who?' I said.
'You', she said.
'Me?' I said.
'Yes', she said.
'Oh'.

*Traditional*

# You're late

'You're late' is a dialogue which comes to a sudden end.

In the development activities that follow, the children make up their own dialogues using words and rhythms.

## Stage 1 · introducing the poem

*(A whole class activity)*

1.   Read the poem to the children and be aware of their reaction to it. They might laugh at the end. Ask the children to suggest possible titles for the poem.
2.   Ask the children what they thought of the ending. Did it seem sudden or unexpected?
3.   Ask the children why the ending seemed sudden or unexpected.

## Stage 2 · making up dialogues

*(An activity to do in pairs)*

In this activity, the children memorize a modified version of 'You're late' and extend it by adding lines of their own.

1.   Divide the children into two large groups (group 1 and group 2) of equal size.
2.   Teach the children this version of the poem in which the groups say alternate lines:

 *Group 1:* **'You're late.'**

*Group 2:* **'Who?'**

 *Group 1:* **'You.'**

*Group 2:* **'Me?'**

 *Group 1:* **'Yes.'**

*Group 2:* **'Oh.'**

3.   Ask each child from group 1 to find a partner from group 2. Ask each pair to practise performing the dialogue they learned in the large groups. Then ask them to make up more lines to delay the sudden ending.

 *1:*   **'You're late.'**

*2:*   **'Who?'**

 *1:*   **'You.'**

*2:*   **'Me?'**

 *1:*   **'Yes.'**

*2:*   **'I'm not late.'**

 *1:*   **'You are.'**

*2:*   **'Oh no I'm not.'**

 *1:*   **'Oh yes you are.'**

*2:*   **'Oh.'**

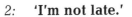
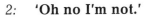

## Stage 3 · making up musical dialogues

*(An activity to do in pairs)*

For this activity, each child continues working with his or her partner from stage 2. Each pair of children make a musical dialogue using the rhythms of the words of the dialogues from stage 2. The children also invent new rhythms to include in their dialogues.

You will need a selection of untuned percussion instruments.

1.  Give one child in each pair an untuned percussion instrument. The child with the instrument will play and the other child will respond with body percussion sounds, such as claps, taps and clicks.

2.  Each pair of children begins its musical dialogue by performing the rhythms of the words of the dialogue made up at stage 2.

 1:

('You're late.')

2:

('Who?')

 1:

('You, of course,')

2:

('I   am   not   late.')

However, instead of saying the words, the child with the instrument plays the rhythm of his or her words, while the other child claps, taps or clicks the rhythm of his or her words.

The result is a musical dialogue made up of rhythms.

3.  The children can develop their musical dialogues further by making up more rhythms to perform. The rhythms performed do not have to correspond to the rhythms of words.

4.  The children can decide between themselves who will end the musical conversation by performing a sudden sound. The ending can be a single sound like the poem's ending.

 1:

('Oh.')

Alternatively, the children can think of other surprising, sudden or unexpected ways to end their dialogues.

5.  Ask some pairs of children to perform their musical conversations to the rest of the class.

**Musical skills and knowledge developed:**
*   **Composing:** inventing rhythms and placing them in a musical structure; devising endings
*   **Duration:** rhythmic patterns
*   **Structure:** phrases; musical dialogues; endings

# The toaster

A silver-scaled Dragon with jaws flaming red
Sits at my elbow and toasts my bread.
I hand him fat slices, and then, one by one,
He hands them back when he sees they are done.

*William Jay Smith*

# The toaster

This poem contains a metaphor - the toaster is described as a dragon.

In the musical development activities, the children make moving sound sculptures of household appliances.

## Stage 1 · introducing the poem

*(A whole class activity)*

1.    The children think of household appliances and discuss their appearances, the purposes for which they are made and their designs.  Include toasters in this discussion.

2.    Read the poem to the children without revealing the title.  Ask them which household appliance is being described in the poem.  Why do they think the toaster is described as though it is a dragon?

3.    Explain what a metaphor is and that the poem contains one.

## Stage 2 · making up vocal sounds

*(A small group activity)*

For this activity, you will need enlarged photocopies of the household appliances and adjectives shown opposite.

The children make up vocal sounds reflecting the household appliances and adjectives.

1.    Divide the class into small groups of five or six.  Allocate to each group one adjective and a photocopied picture of a household appliance.  A group might have any pairing of adjective and household appliance, such as 'sad vacuum cleaner' or 'fierce corkscrew'.

2.    The groups consider all the functions of their appliances and the activities that surround them.  The children in each group then make up vocal sounds imitating their household appliance, but also capturing the mood of the describing word.

## Stage 3 · making a moving sound sculpture

*(A small group activity)*

In this activity, the groups make movements with their sounds.  The movements should reflect the sounds, the appliance and the adjective.

The children remain in the same groups they were in for stage 2.

1.    Discuss with the whole class how movements can reflect sounds.  Ask the children to consider whether the movements they will perform with their sounds should be:
•    fast or slow;
•    large or small;
•    performed once or repeated several times.

The children should also consider:
•    which part or parts of the body should be used for the movements;
•    whether the body should imitate the shape of the appliance;
•    whether they should travel with the movement;
•    whether the movement should be performed before, with or after the sound.

2.  The groups think of suitable movements to go with the vocal sounds they thought of in stage 2.

3.  Each group now organises its movements and sounds into a sequence in order to make a moving sound sculpture of the described household appliance. Encourage the children to be imaginative about how they do this.

4.  Each group performs its moving sound sculpture for the rest of the class.

**Musical skills and knowledge developed:**

*   **Composing:** inventing vocal sounds and organising them for a performance
*   **Movement:** devising movements that reflect sounds and organising them for a performance
*   **Timbre:** exploring varieties of sound colours
*   **Duration:** long and short sounds
*   **Pitch:** high and low sounds

Lawn mower

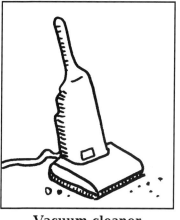

Food mixer

Vacuum cleaner

**Angry**

**Lazy**

**Fierce**

**Busy**

**Sad**

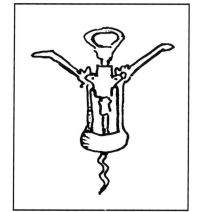

Corkscrew

Broom

Toaster

**Nervous**

# The swing (Moods of life)

Oopar niche .. tu ichko kai
                  tu ichko kai

Oopar niche .. oo ichko kam
                  oo ichko kam

      Tu ichko kai
      oo ichko kam

Oopar niche .. tu ichko kai
Oopar niche .. oo ichko kam

      Tu ichko kai
      Oo ichko kam
      Oo ichko kam
      Tu ichko kai

Oopar niche ..
Niche oopar

Oo ichko kam
Oo ichko kam
Tu ichko kai
Tu ichko kai

Oopar niche .. niche oopar
Oopar niche .. niche oopar

Oo ichko kam
Tu ichko kai
Tu ichko kai
Tu ichko kai
Tu ichko kai
    Tu ichko kai
    Tu ichko kai
    Oo ichko kam

*Mary D. Chauhan*

# The swing (Moods of life)

This poem consists of three lines which recur throughout, written phonetically in the language of Gujerati. The first two phrases 'Oopar niche .. tu ichko kai' translate literally as 'Up down ... you are swinging'.

In the development activities, the children make up spoken ostinatos and musical ostinatos. An ostinato is a pattern of sounds repeated over and over again.

## Stage 1 · introducing the poem

*(A whole class activity)*

Familiarise yourself with the poem. Find a way of reciting the words that you feel comfortable with and that fits with a steady beat.

1.   Read the poem to the children. Ask them if they can remember any lines from the poem or if they noticed any words or lines being repeated.

2.   Explain that there are three lines that are repeated throughout the poem but that they are not repeated according to a fixed pattern. Show this by asking the class to push an imaginary person on a swing when they hear the word 'Oopar'. Because this word is not repeated at regular intervals, the class will have to listen carefully for when it occurs.

## Stage 2 · making a spoken ostinato

*(A whole class activity)*

In stage 1, the children learned that although the lines of 'The swing (Moods of life)' were repeated throughout the poem, they were not repeated according to a fixed pattern. In this activity, the children make a pattern out of the poem lines, then repeat them over and over again to make a spoken ostinato.

1.   Chant the three poem lines with the children.

**Oopar niche**
**tu ichko kai**
**oo ichko kam**

Accompany the children with a steady drum beat, played in time with the chanting.

2.   Ask one child to make a short pattern out of the three lines. The child places the lines in an order. The child can choose to include a line more than once in the pattern, or omit a line.

Here are some example patterns:

**tu ichko kai - oopar niche -**
**- oo ichko kam - tu ichko kai.**

**oo ichko kam - oo ichko kam - tu ichko kai.**

3.   The class chants the pattern made by the child over and over again. This is a spoken ostinato.

Ask other children to make new patterns made from the three lines. The class can chant these suggested patterns several times, and then choose its favourite pattern to be the spoken ostinato used in stage 3.

# Stage 3 - adding instrumental ostinatos to the spoken ostinato

*(A whole class activity)*

In this activity, the children make up musical ostinatos using instruments while the spoken ostinato from stage 2 is chanted.

You will need untuned percussion instruments. If possible, the children should sit in a circle.

1.    The children take turns to listen to the spoken ostinato from stage 2, while making up new patterns to repeat over and over again.

The patterns the children make up should:
*   be different from the pattern made by the words but fit with the steady drum beat;
*   sound pleasing with the spoken ostinato;
*   be short and simple enough for the children to be able to repeat over and over again.

The children can practise their patterns by tapping them on their knees, while listening to the spoken ostinato.

2.    Give an untuned percussion instrument to the first child in the circle. Ask the class to begin chanting the spoken ostinato. Play a steady drum beat in time with the spoken ostinato. While the spoken ostinato is chanted, the child with the instrument plays the pattern he or she tapped.

The child with the instrument may need to spend a few moments establishing his or her instrumental ostinato. The rest of the class should continue chanting the spoken ostinato with the steady drum beat.

When the child has played his or her ostinato, the instrument is passed on to the next child.

3.    Give instruments to two or three children spaced around the circle. The children with the instruments play their ostinatos at the same time, while the other children chant the spoken ostinato. The children with the instruments pass them on to the next children in the circle when you give a signal.

**Musical skills and knowledge developed:**
*   **Composing:** making up vocal and instrumental ostinatos
*   **Duration:** rhythmic patterns; steady beat
*   **Texture:** layers of sounds
*   **Structure:** ostinatos

---

**An example plan showing the drum beat, a spoken ostinato and two instrumental ostinatos**

| | |
|---|---|
| *Drum beat:* | |
| *1st ostinato:* | |
| *2nd ostinato:*<br>*Spoken ostinato:* | <br>**Oopar niche - oo ichko kam   - tu ichko kai;   Oopar niche - oo ichko kam   - tu ichko kai;** |

# The song the train sang

This...is...the...one...
That...is...the...one...
This is the one,
That is the one,
This is the one, that is the one
This is the one, that is the one...

Over the river, past the mill,
Through the tunnel under the hill;
Round the corner, past the wall,
Through the wood where trees grow tall.
Then in sight of the town by the river,
Brake by the crossing where white leaves quiver.
Slow as the streets of the town slide past
And the windows stare
   at the jerking of the coaches
  Coming into the station approaches.

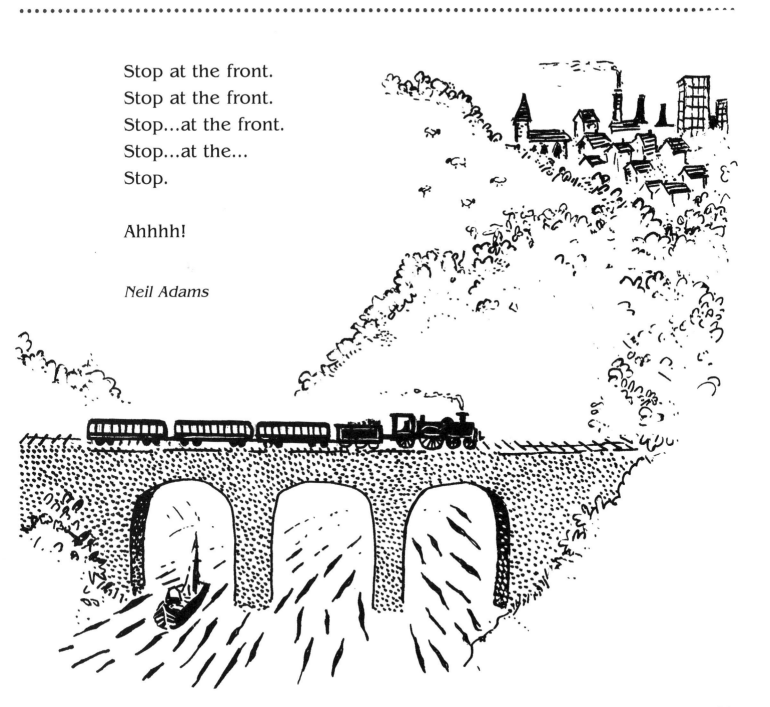

Stop at the front.
Stop at the front.
Stop...at the front.
Stop...at the...
Stop.

Ahhhh!

*Neil Adams*

# The song the train sang

This extract from the poem 'The song the train sang' describes three stages in the journey of a steam train - gathering momentum, full motion and slowing down to a stop.

In the musical development activities, the children invent and select sounds that remind them of steam trains. They organise the sounds into short pieces of music.

## Stage 1 · introducing the poem

*(A whole class activity)*

In this activity, the children guess the subject of the poem by listening to it.

When you read the extract to the children, emphasize the different speeds. Start the poem very slowly and heavily, gradually getting faster. Chant the middle section with a steady, regular beat as the train travels at full speed. Then slow down gradually as the train does until you come to a stop.

1.    Do not tell the class anything about the poem before you read it. Read it with the changes of pace described above. Ask the children to suggest possible titles for the poem.

2.    Ask the children how they knew what the poem was about. (At no point is the word 'train' mentioned in the poem.)

## Stage 2 · making up steam train music

*(A small group activity)*

Have available some untuned percussion instruments that the children can use if they wish.

1.    Discuss with the class the sounds a steam train might make in full motion. Does the steam train or parts of it, such as the doors or seats, make sounds that:
- have definite rhythms or patterns;
- are repetitive;
- change if, for example, the train goes through a tunnel?

2.    Divide the class into small groups of four or five. Each group thinks of sounds and patterns of sounds it associates with steam trains travelling in full motion. These can be vocal, body percussion or instrumental sounds.

Encourage the groups to be adventurous in their choice of sounds. The sounds should be varied. Some should be repeating sounds; others may only need to be performed once.

3.    Each group finds ways to fit their sounds together to make a short piece of music which reflects the motion of a moving steam train. All the pieces should have a steady beat.

There are various ways in which the children in each group might try to fit their sounds together, such as taking turns in the group to perform the sounds individually, performing sounds in pairs, or overlapping sounds to make interesting effects.

4.    When the groups have developed their pieces of music, each group performs to the rest of the class.

# Stage 3 · developing the steam train music

*(A whole class activity)*

In this activity, the short pieces of music made up in stage 2 and the first and last sections of the poem extract are joined together to make a class performance.

There are three sections to practise separately before the whole piece of music can be performed.

1.   First practise chanting the first section of the poem in which the train speeds up.  You and the children chant the words together, getting gradually faster.  The children may tap or clap the rhythm of the words as they chant them.

2.   In the same way, practise chanting the last section of the poem, getting gradually slower.

3.   The middle section is a combination of the group pieces.  You need to decide the order in which the groups will perform and establish start and stop signals that the children will respond to.

4.   Signal to the first group to start performing its piece of music.  Then, while the first group is still performing, signal to the second group to begin its piece - the music overlaps.  You then signal to the first group to stop performing.  Signal to the third group to begin.  Continue this process until all the groups have performed.

5.   Practise linking all three sections of the performance.  When the last group has performed its piece of music for sufficient time, signal to everyone to begin the final section ('Stop at the front').  At this moment, the last group ends its piece of music.

6.   When everyone can confidently perform and link all three sections, try a whole performance.

**Musical skills and knowledge developed:**
*   **Composing:** making vocal, body percussion and instrumental sounds and organising them into a piece of music
*   **Tempo:** getting faster and slower
*   **Timbre:** using different sound qualities
*   **Structure:** beginning, contrasting middle, end

# Seashore

Pretty shells washed onto the sand,
Sand a golden yellow colour,
Colour in the blue of the sea,
Sea with gentle lapping waves,
Waves clouded with green seaweed,
Seaweed clinging to the breakwaters.
Breakwaters stand ugly in the water,
Water envelops the cliffs,
Cliffs with bare white faces.
Faces of donkeys and faces of people,
People lying tanned in deckchairs,

Deckchairs lying disregarded.
Disregarded boats tied to the piers,
Piers standing rooted in pebbles,
Pebbles worn smooth by the water,
Water collecting in the rock pools.
Rock pools inhabited by limpets,
Limpets stuck to surrounding rocks,
Rocks distorted like bits of wood,
Wood washed up along the shore,
Shore with litter, synthetic rope.

*Nadya Kassam*

# Seashore

The last word of each line of 'Seashore' is the first word of the next line. Because of the way the lines link with each other, we have called it a 'chain poem'. The lines of 'Talk war' on page 10 link in the same way.

In the musical activities, the children make up 'chain music' using phrases of pitched notes that follow a structure comparable to that of the 'chain poem'. ('Chain music' is not technically a musical term.)

## Stage 1 · introducing the poem and exploring its structure

*(A whole class activity)*

The children explore the chain structure through a simple activity. You will need twenty-one large strips of card, each with one line of the poem written on it.

Pretty shells washed onto the sand,

Sand a golden yellow colour,

Colour in the blue of the sea,

1.   Read the poem to the class. Discuss with the children what they remember described in the poem.

2.   Prepare to explore the structure of the poem. Randomly give out the strips of card to the children. You may need to allocate some cards to pairs of children in order to involve everyone in this activity.

3.   Read out the first line of the poem and ask which child has the card with this line on it. This child (or pair of children) stands up and reads the line. You now ask who has the card that begins with the last word of that line, ('sand'). The child with the card goes to stand next to the first child, then reads his or her line.

This process is continued until all the children are standing with their cards in the order in which the lines occur in the poem.

4.   When the children are standing with their lines in the correct order, they can read the whole chain poem.

## Stage 2 · improvising chain music

*(A small group activity)*

In this activity, the children improvise a chain of musical phrases. Each phrase begins on the last note of the previous phrase.

The children must listen to and watch each other carefully so that they know which note was the last note of the musical phrase.

1.    Divide the children into groups of five or six. Give each group a glockenspiel, a xylophone or a set of five chime bars tuned to C, D, E, G and A. Give one child in each group two beaters. If you feel it necessary, give the children an order to play in by numbering them from 1 - 6.

2.    The child with the beaters makes up a short musical phrase using the notes available. When the child has finished playing, he or she passes the beaters on to the next child in the group.

3.    The child who now has the beaters makes up a short musical phrase. This phrase must begin on the last note of the previous phrase. Here are some example phrases:

| | |
|---|---|
| *1st child's phrase:* | **C EE G A  G** |
| *2nd child's phrase:* | **G E  D  CC E** |
| *3rd child's phrase:* | **EE EE AGAG C** |

4.    The children continue this process until everyone in the group has had several attempts at making up a musical phrase for the piece of chain music.

## Stage 3 - refining ideas for a chain composition

*(A small group activity)*

When the children are familiar with the stage 2 process of making up chain music, they can refine and develop their ideas to make chain compositions.

1.    In stage 2, the children freely improvised phrases to make chain music. Some of the phrases that they improvised may not have sounded satisfactory. The children should now refine their phrases. They consider with more care how their phrases sound as part of a composition. Ask them to work on making up phrases that sound pleasing when performed after each other. Ask the children to think carefully about how their phrases relate to each other, perhaps by having similar rhythms or note patterns.

2.    Each group discusses their ideas for relating the phrases. Then each child works individually on a phrase for the group's chain composition.

Remind the children that the phrases must form a chain - the first note of a phrase must be the last note of the previous phrase.

3.    The groups try performing their phrases in order for their chain composition. They may find it necessary to adapt, improve or refine some of their phrases in order to include them in the final composition.

4.    When each child has contributed one or more phrases to his or her group's chain composition and the groups are satisfied with their compositions, (including how they begin and end), the groups can perform their compositions to the rest of the class.

**Musical skills and knowledge developed:**

- **Composing:** making up phrases using pitched notes; fitting the phrases into a structure; refining phrases for a composition
- **Pitch:** selecting notes to use in phrases; beginning phrases on specific pitches
- **Structure:** phrases

# The last exam
**A villanelle**

To read the questions carefully
I hold my breath like a balloon.
After this one I'll be free

of European History,
of desks and people in this room,
after this one I'll be free.

'In the thirteenth century...'
It's much too hot this afternoon
to read the questions carefully.

I watch them scribble busily
as if there were no flaming June...
after this one I'll be free

to fish and swim down by the sea,
to lie and dream or watch the moon.
To read the questions carefully,

and answer them, I have to be
a wingless bug in a cocoon.
After this one I'll be free

to fly and make some history.
So I begin, in silent gloom,
to read the questions carefully.
After this one I'll be free.

*Jane Whittle*

# The last exam

## A villanelle

'The last exam' is a villanelle. Villanelle is a strict verse form of poetry dating from the Middle Ages. It features repetition and contrast.

Each stanza contains three lines, except the last which contains four. The first stanza introduces two lines which are repeated in the poem. In the outline of the form below, these lines are called 'line A' and 'line B'. The other lines of the poem are all different and do not repeat. They are called 'free lines' in the outline below.

| | | |
|---|---|---|
| **Stanza 1** | Line A | *To read the questions carefully* |
| | Free line | I hold my breath like a balloon. |
| | Line B | *After this one I'll be free* |
| | | |
| **Stanza 2** | Free line | of European History, |
| | Free line | of desks and people in this room, |
| | Line B | *after this one I'll be free.* |
| | | |
| **Stanza 3** | Free line | 'In the thirteenth century...' |
| | Free line | It's much too hot this afternoon |
| | Line A | *to read the questions carefully.* |
| | | |
| **Stanza 4** | Free line | I watch them scribble busily |
| | Free line | as if there were no flaming June... |
| | Line B | *after this one I'll be free* |
| | | |
| **Stanza 5** | Free line | to fish and swim down by the sea, |
| | Free line | to lie and dream or watch the moon. |
| | Line A | *To read the questions carefully,* |
| | | |
| **Stanza 6** | Free line | and answer them, I have to be |
| | Free line | a wingless bug in a cocoon. |
| | Line B | *After this one I'll be free* |
| | | |
| **Last stanza** | Free line | to fly and make some history. |
| | Free line | So I begin, in silent gloom, |
| | Line A | *to read the questions carefully.* |
| | Line B | *After this one I'll be free.* |

In the activities, the children explore the villanelle and make up pieces of music that follow its structure.

## Stage 1 · introducing the poem and villanelle form

*(A whole class activity)*

In this activity, the children work out which lines in the poem recur and when they recur. Before beginning, photocopy and enlarge the pictures below and paste them separately on to cards. Make thirteen 'free line' cards, four 'line A' cards and five 'line B' cards. There should be twenty-two cards altogether.

1.   Read the poem to the children and discuss their reactions.

2.   Explain that the poem is a villanelle. In a villanelle the lines follow a strict pattern in which two lines recur several times. Read 'The last exam' again. Can anyone identify the two recurring lines?

3.   When the children have spotted the two recurring lines, prepare to explore when the lines are repeated in the poem. Introduce the three groups of cards, explaining which line or lines each represents.

4.   The children listen to the poem and put the cards in order.

Read the first line of the poem. Ask a child to come to the front, choose the correct card and hold it. Continue reading, pausing after each line to ask a child to choose the card which represents the line. The children line up holding their cards in the order that matches the lines of the poem. The resulting pattern shows the structure of the lines of the villanelle.

(The cards should finish up in the order of the poem lines shown opposite in the explanation of the villanelle form.)

'Line A'

'Free line'

'Line B'

## Stage 2 · performing repeated and contrasting rhythms

*(A whole class activity)*

In this activity, the children repeat rhythms you play to them, or invent contrasting ones, depending on whether you give the instruction 'repeat' or 'change'.

If possible, the children sit in a circle. Make sure that everyone can see everyone else. You will need two untuned percussion instruments. You keep one of the instruments while the other is passed around the circle.

1.  Explain to the class that the child holding the instrument will either repeat a rhythm that you play on your instrument, or will invent something different to play, depending on whether you say 'repeat' or 'change'.

2.  The first child with the instrument in the circle listens to your instruction followed by the rhythm you play on your instrument. According to your instruction, the child either plays your rhythm back to you or invents something different. He or she then passes the instrument on to the next child in the circle.

You can choose to change your own rhythm each time you play for a different child. Make sure that the rhythms you perform are of an appropriate length for your pupils to be able to remember.

3.  Finish this activity when all the children have had turns to copy your rhythm and to invent different rhythms.

## Stage 3 · composing a piece of music in the structure of the villanelle

*(A small group activity)*

In this activity, the children make up a piece of music following a shortened version of the villanelle structure, using five verses only.

The children make up two musical phrases that recur in the same way that the two lines in the villanelle recur. They also make up contrasting musical phrases which are not repeated.

Make several enlarged photocopies of the plan of the structure shown opposite. It shows how the musical phrases should be organised. The two repeating phrases are marked 'A' and 'B'; the free phrases are not marked.

1.  Divide the children into small groups of four or five. Give each group one tuned and one untuned percussion instrument and a photocopy of the plan of the structure.

2.  The children in each group devise two simple musical phrases which they can remember and repeat easily. One is played on the untuned percussion instrument, the other on the tuned instrument.

3.  The group decides which of its two repeating phrases will be represented by the 'phrase A' and 'phrase B' symbols. The group also decides which of its members will be responsible for playing each of these phrases in the piece of music. They write

the names of the players on the plan of the structure in the appropriate places.

4.   Each group then thinks of contrasting ideas for the free phrases which will not be repeated. These phrases can be played on the tuned or untuned percussion instruments, or can be made up of body percussion or vocal sounds.

5.   The group decides which of its members will play the free phrases.  As there are several of them, the group members may want to take it in turns to perform.

The group writes the name of each player on to the plan of the structure in the appropriate places.

6.   When the groups have had ample time to practise and refine their compositions, ask them to perform them for the rest of the class.

**Musical skills and knowledge developed:**
- **Composing:** making up repeating phrases and contrasting phrases; fitting phrases into a structure
- **Performing:** performing phrases at the correct point in a structure
- **Structure:** phrases; repetition

## Plan of the villanelle structure

| (A) | |
| --- | --- |
| | |
| (B) | |

| | |
| --- | --- |
| | |
| (B) | |

| | |
| --- | --- |
| | |
| (A) | |

| | |
| --- | --- |
| | |
| (B) | |

| | |
| --- | --- |
| | |
| (A) | |
| (B) | |

# Mama Dot

Born on a sunday
in the kingdom of Ashante

Sold on monday
into slavery

Ran away on tuesday
cause she born free

Lost a foot on wednesday
when they catch she

Worked all thursday
till her head grey

Dropped on friday
where they burned she

Freed on saturday
in a new century

*Fred D'Aguiar*

# Mama Dot

In this poem, Fred D'Aguiar describes Mama Dot's life with seven brief statements, each associated with a day of the week. There is a gradual build-up of tension throughout the poem until finally, Mama Dot is freed by death.

In the musical development activities, the children explore and develop different musical accompaniments for the poem.

## Stage 1 - introducing the poem

*(A whole class activity)*

In this activity, the children discuss the poem and recite it.

1. Read the poem to the class. Ask the children what they noticed about it. Did they notice the seven days of the week? Did they notice the build-up of tension?

2. Divide the children into seven groups and allocate a stanza to each. When each group has memorized its stanza, ask the groups to perform the poem by reciting the stanzas in order.

## Stage 2 - performing simple accompaniments for the poem

*(Small group and whole class activities)*

For this stage, the children perform two very simple accompaniments as they recite the poem. The children remain in their groups from stage 1.

Have available a selection of chime bars tuned to any notes.

1. Ask one child from each of the seven groups to choose a chime bar.

2. The child with the chime bar plays one note before his or her group recites its stanza. The note can be as long, short, loud or quiet as the child feels is appropriate. Each group can decide whether to recite its stanza while the sound of the note rings on, or whether to wait until the note has finished.

Ask all seven groups to recite the stanzas in order and play the simple chime bar accompaniment.

3. Try developing the accompaniment by building up the sound of the chime bar notes. (At this point, you may wish to give other children in the groups the opportunity to play the chime bars.) Organise the seven chime bar players so that the first child plays before the first stanza, the first and second children play before the second stanza, the first, second and third children play before the third stanza, and so on, until all seven children play before the seventh stanza.

4. The children with the chime bars practise playing their notes at the same time. You can conduct the players or signal to them to play their notes. Alternatively, the players can watch an appointed leader so that they know when to play.

(At this point, the chime bar players can work on how the notes are performed. The notes can be loud or quiet, long or short.)

5. When the chime bar players have practised playing together, the class recites the poem with the new musical accompaniment.

# Stage 3 · developing a new accompaniment for the poem

*(Small group and whole class activities)*

For this stage, the children select percussion instruments to use in a new musical accompaniment for the poem.

Have available a selection of tuned and untuned percussion instruments.

As for stage 2, the children need to be in seven groups, each of which recites one stanza of the poem. You may wish to regroup the children or reallocate the stanzas of the poem before proceeding.

1.  Explain to the children that, as before, one sound will be performed for each stanza of the poem. However, this time each group selects the tuned or untuned percussion instrument it thinks will sound effective with its verse.

Give each group some time to explore the various sounds made by the instruments before choosing one. Then choose seven children, one from each group, to be the instrument players.

2.  Each group decides when their percussion sound will be performed during the stanza. The sound does not have to be at the beginning.

**Born on a sunday**

**in the kingdom of Ashante**

The groups experiment with playing sounds at different points during their stanzas. Each group

decides whether its percussion sound should either:

*   help emphasize an important word, or,
*   be heard in between words, or,
*   be heard before or after the stanza.

3.  The players also decide how their sounds should be performed. Ask each player to consider how his or her sound should be played in order to be most effective. It can be:

*   loud, quiet, or in between;
*   long, short, or in between;
*   high, low, or in between (if a pitched sound).

**Born on a sunday**

**in the kingdom of Ashante**

The children can also experiment with their instruments to produce unusual sounds.

4.  When each group has practised its stanza and accompanying sound, the class can perform the whole poem with the new musical accompaniment.

**Musical skills and knowledge developed:**

*   **Composing:** using single sounds to make an accompaniment; deciding how to perform sounds; choosing effective moments to perform sounds
*   **Texture:** performing several sounds at once
*   **Pitch, duration, dynamics, timbre:** using the elements effectively to capture the mood of the words

# Two haiku

Poem in three lines:
Five syllables, then seven,
Five again; no rhyme.

*Eric Finney*

'Syllable writing,
Counting out your seventeen,
Doesn't produce poem.

Good haiku need thought:
One simple statement followed
By poet's comment.

The town dump is white
With seagulls, like butterflies
Over a garden.'

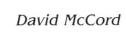

*David McCord*

# The woodland haiku

*Fox*
Slinks to the wood's edge
and - with one paw raised - surveys
the open meadows.

*Fallow deer*
Moves as smooth as smoke
and starts at an air tremor.
Is gone like a ghost.

*Rabbits*
Blind panic sets in
and they're off; dodgem cars
gone out of control.

*Rooks*
They float high above,
black as scraps of charred paper
drifting from a fire.

*Owl*
*Blip* on his radar
sends owl whooshing through the dark,
homing in on mice, rats.

*Pike*
Killer submarine
he lurks deep in the woodland's
green-skinned pond.  Lurks ... waits.

*Sheep's skull*
Whitened and toothless,
discovered in a damp ditch.
A trophy for home.

*Humans*
Clumsy, twig-snapping,
they see nothing but trees, trees.
The creatures hide ... watch ...

*Wes Magee*

# Haiku
# The woodland haiku

Haiku (pronounced high-coo) is a traditional Japanese form of poetry which uses seventeen syllables divided into three lines. The first and last lines each have five syllables and the middle line has seven.

Eric Finney's haiku on page 41 describes haiku form. David McCord's haiku on the same page describes what makes a good haiku. In Wes Magee's poem 'The woodland haiku' on pages 42-43, each haiku describes an animal.

In the musical development activities, the children compose musical accompaniments for haiku from the poem 'The woodland haiku'.

## Stage 1 - introducing haiku

*(A whole class activity)*

In this section, the children find out about haiku.

You will need five red cards, seven yellow cards and five blue cards, all with white backs.

1.    Read Eric Finney's poem on page 41. Explain that it describes haiku, and if necessary, explain what a syllable is.

2.    Show the children that Eric Finney's poem is a haiku.

Place your coloured cards face down in three lines. Slowly read the first line of the poem, turning over a red card for each syllable. Ask the children how many syllables there were. Repeat this process with the yellow cards for the second line and the blue cards for the third line. By counting the syllables with the help of the cards, the children can deduce that the poem itself is a haiku.

3.    Read David McCord's haiku on page 41 to the children. Tell them that it is a haiku about how to write good haiku.

4.    At this stage you could give the children the opportunity to write their own haiku on subjects of their own choice. Ask some children to read out their haiku. Check that the haiku have the correct number of lines and syllables.

## Stage 2 - choosing sounds to accompany haiku

*(A small group activity)*

In this activity, the children choose sounds they feel are suitable to accompany a haiku from 'The woodland haiku'.

Have available a selection of tuned and untuned percussion instruments.

1.    Read 'The woodland haiku' to the children and discuss their reactions to it.

2.    Divide the children into small groups of four or five. Each group chooses a haiku from the poem for which it will make up a musical accompaniment.

3.    Help each group to memorize its chosen haiku by reading it to them several times.

4.    Each group discusses the characteristics of the animal featured in its chosen haiku, such as the way it moves, its habitat, its appearance, or its fur, scales, skin or feathers. Each group then considers

what sounds will reflect these characteristics.

Ask each group whether its sounds should be:
- long or short;
- high or low;
- loud, quiet, or getting louder or quieter.

The groups should also consider the colour or 'timbre' of the sounds they choose. They may need to consider the relative suitability of sounds, such as whether a triangle is more appropriate than a coco-rattle.

The sounds chosen can be vocal sounds, body percussion sounds, sounds made by instruments or any combination of these. Encourage the children to be imaginative in their choice of sounds; you may want to discourage them from merely imitating the sound made by the animal.

5.    The children in each group work together to find between five and seven sounds or patterns of sounds that reflect the characteristics of the animal in their chosen poem. The children will use these sounds to make up a musical accompaniment in stage 3.

## Stage 3 - organising sounds into musical accompaniments for 'The woodland haiku'

*(A small group activity)*

For this activity, the children remain in the same groups as for stage 2. They organise the sounds they chose in stage 2 into a musical accompaniment for their haiku.

1.    Each group considers how it will use its chosen sounds effectively to make an accompaniment for its haiku.

Tell the children that the sounds can be:
- performed more than once;
- grouped into phrases;
- performed as single sounds or combined with other sounds to make clusters of sounds;
- performed before, after or at the same time as the words of the haiku;
- used to emphasize important words of the haiku.

2.    The groups practise reciting their chosen haiku while trying out different ways of performing their musical sounds. Each group should try to be imaginative about how it performs the musical sounds with the haiku. The groups consider what effects they would like to achieve and organise their sounds into accompaniments.

3.    When the groups have composed their musical accompaniments, they perform them with their haiku for the rest of the class.

4.    Ask the children to explain what they thought was effective about their musical accompaniments.

**Musical skills and knowledge developed:**
- **Composing:** selecting and organising a small number of sounds for a musical accompaniment
- **Pitch, duration, dynamics, tempo, timbre, texture, structure:** using the elements effectively to make a musical accompaniment that complements the words of the haiku

# I'm a hip hoppy kid

I'm a hip hoppy kid and you'll never catch me nappin,
No matter where I go you'll always hear me rappin...
I rap to the east and I rap to the west...
I rap in my socks and I rap in my vest...
I rap in my sleep and drive the neighbours potty...
I rap in the bathroom when I'm drying off my botty...
I rap to the birds and I rap to the bees...
And when I go completely daft I rap to the trees...
I can even rap on wheels, I really am the master...
I wish I'd seen that manhole then I wouldn't be in plaster...

*Kirtiss Horswell*

# I'm a hip hoppy kid

'I'm a hip hoppy kid' is a rap. The words have an energetic rhythm and should be performed with a steady beat. In this rap, the last words of each pair of lines rhyme. Raps do not have to follow this rhyming scheme, though many do.

In the following activities, the children write their own raps and musical accompaniments.

## Stage 1 · introducing the rap

*(A whole class activity)*

1.   Read the rap to the whole group. Do the children know what kind of a poem it is? Discuss raps with the children.

2.   Read the rap again. Ask everyone to join in by tapping, clicking or clapping the beat.

## Stage 2 · making up raps

*(A small group activity)*

1.   Divide the children into small groups. Ask each group to make up words for a short rap.

2.   When the groups have made up words for their raps, ask each of them to perform for the rest of the class. Encourage each group to clap, click or tap the beat as it performs.

## Stage 3 · developing the performances of the raps

*(A small group activity)*

For this stage, the groups develop their raps and find ways to make them more exciting by devising musical accompaniments.

Have available a selection of tuned and untuned percussion instruments. Electronic keyboards can also be used effectively, if available.

1.   Each group makes up an accompaniment for its rap by using body percussion sounds and instrumental sounds.

The groups can:
*   play on the beat;
*   make patterns of sounds to repeat over and over again;
*   perform particular sounds at special or appropriate moments in the rap;
*   develop their performance by finding moments to pause between words while the accompaniment sounds carry on.

2.   Each group organises its performance. The children need to decide who will perform accompanying sounds and who will perform the words of the rap.

(Use a microphone if you have one available. It will help to exaggerate the sounds of the words and make accompanying vocal effects such as tongue clicks or popping sounds more exciting.)

**Musical skills and knowledge developed:**
*   **Composing:** making up a rhythmic accompaniment for a rap
*   **Duration:** rhythmic patterns; steady beat
*   **Timbre:** exploring sounds for the accompaniment

# Don't call alligator long-mouth till you cross river

Call alligator long-mouth
call alligator saw-mouth
call alligator pushy-mouth
call alligator scissors-mouth
call alligator raggedy-mouth
call alligator bumpy-bum
call alligator all dem rude word
but better wait
       till you cross river.

*John Agard*

# Don't call alligator long-mouth till you cross river

This short poem contains several insulting names for an alligator.

In the musical development activities, the children compose sections of music capturing the mood of the insults. The sections are then linked together to make a piece of music.

## Stage 1 - introducing the poem

*(Whole class activities)*

If possible, the children sit in a large circle. The children will hear the poem, improvise new names to describe the alligator and participate in a performance of the poem.

1.    Read the poem to the children. Which names used to describe the alligator can the children remember?

2.    Ask each child to make up one new name for the alligator. Each child will say his or her alligator name after you say 'call alligator'.

You say 'call alligator'. Then the first child in the circle says his or her alligator name. Say 'call alligator' again and the next child in the circle says his or her name. Continue this process until every child has contributed a name.

Try to avoid gaps between your 'call alligator' line and the names said by the children.

3.    Divide the circle of children into seven groups. Choose confident children for group 1. Then allocate the words of the poem as follows:

| | |
|---|---|
| *Group 1:* | **Call alligator** |
| *Group 2:* | **long-mouth** |
| *Group 3:* | **saw-mouth** |
| *Group 4:* | **pushy-mouth** |
| *Group 5:* | **scissors-mouth** |
| *Group 6:* | **raggedy-mouth** |
| *Group 7:* | **bumpy-bum** |
| *Groups 2-7:* | **all dem rude word** |
| *Group 1:* | **but better wait till you cross river** |

4.    When the groups are confident of their words, they participate in a performance of the poem. Group 1 begins followed by group 2. Group 1 then says its words again, and must remember to do so seven times in total before each name called out by the other groups. When group 1 has said 'call alligator' for the last time, groups 2-7 say 'all dem rude word' before group 1 concludes with the last line of the poem.

## Stage 2 - making up sections of 'alligator music'

*(A small group activity)*

For this activity, the children remain in the seven groups they were in for the class performance of the poem in stage 1. The groups make up sections of music to reflect the words of the poem.

Have available a selection of tuned and untuned percussion instruments.

1.    Explain that each group is to make up a short section of music.

Groups 2-7 use the poem words allocated to them as the starting points for their sections of music. The music made up by each group should reflect the mood of its expression.

For the 'call alligator' music, group 1 can make up music reflecting an alligator's journey along a river. Group 1 must also make up a different section of music to reflect the last line of the poem to end the composition.

2.  The groups choose instruments for their sections of music. Ask each group of children to consider what qualities its piece of music should have to reflect the mood of the expression.

3.  The groups compose their sections of music. The sections can be as long or short as you and the children feel is appropriate.

## Stage 3 - joining up the sections of 'alligator music'

*(A whole class activity)*

In this activity, the sections of music made up by the small groups in stage 2 are linked together to make one piece of music.

If possible, find a large space in which to do this activity.

1.  Organise the seven groups so that they can all see both you and each other. If possible, group 1 should be in the centre of the room. Explain that the groups will perform their sections of music in a particular order to make a piece of music.

2.  The groups play in the following order:

Group 1 plays the 'call alligator' music. When group 1 stops playing, group 2 ('long-mouth')

plays its music. Group 1 then plays the 'call alligator' music again, followed by group 3 ('saw-mouth') playing its music. This pattern is continued until group 7 ('bumpy-bum') has performed its music. After this group 1 then performs the section of music it composed in stage 2 for the final line of the poem.

3.  Give the class opportunities to practise performing the links between sections so that there are no unexpected hesitations.

4.  Ask the class to perform the piece of music all the way through.

**Musical skills and knowledge developed:**

- **Composing:** choosing sounds and organising them into a piece of music reflecting the mood of the poem
- **Pitch, duration, dynamics, tempo, timbre and texture:** using the musical elements to achieve an intended effect
- **Structure:** returning sections and contrasting sections of music

# The leader

I wanna be the leader
I wanna be the leader
Can I be the leader?
Can I?  I can?
Promise?  Promise?
Yippee, I'm the leader
I'm the leader

OK what shall we do?

*Roger McGough*

# The leader

Roger McGough creates tension in 'The leader' by using three techniques - repeating phrases, repeating parts of phrases and shortening the length of phrases. After the build-up of tension, the last line ends the poem in an unexpected manner.

In the musical development activities, the children make up music that builds up tension and ends in an unexpected manner. To do this, they use the techniques employed by Roger McGough in 'The leader'.

## Stage 1 · introducing the poem

*(A whole class activity)*

In this activity, the children are invited to think of possible endings for the poem. They also explore the build-up of tension during the poem.

1.   Read the poem to the children, leaving out the last line. Reflect the build-up of tension in it by allowing your voice to get louder, faster or higher.

Ask the children to think of occasions when they, or someone they know, has pleaded in a similar way, for example, for an icecream or a turn on a computer.

2.   Read the poem again leaving out the last line. Ask the children what they think the leader might say next.

Read the poem a few times, replacing the last line each time with the children's suggestions.

3.   Now read the poem with Roger McGough's last line. Discuss the children's responses to it.

4.   Discuss the build up of tension in the poem. Ask the children:
*   whether they listen to it wondering if the child will be allowed to be the leader;
*   whether the children think the child in the poem has ever been the leader before;
*   whether the poem becomes more exciting as it progresses.

5.   Discuss how the build-up of tension throughout the poem is achieved.

Show the children how Roger McGough repeats some phrases and varies the length of others. Point out the phrases that are repeated, the parts of phrases that are repeated and the way they become shorter.

Discuss the ways in which you can read the poem to make it exciting, for example, by making your voice get louder, higher, or faster. Sounds that become higher, faster or louder can also create a build-up of tension in music.

## Stage 2 · making up musical dialogues that build up tension

*(An activity to do in pairs)*

In this activity, the children apply the techniques discussed in stage 1 to phrases of music.

1.   Divide the children into pairs. Give each pair either two tuned or two untuned percussion instruments.

2.   The children take it in turns to play musical phrases. They should aim to make up a piece of

music containing between twelve and sixteen musical phrases.

The musical dialogues should build up tension. To do this, the children can employ the techniques used by Roger McGough in his poem:

- repeating phrases;
- repeating parts of phrases;
- shortening the lengths of phrases.

The children can also build up tension by composing music that gets:

- higher;
- louder;
- faster.

3.   Give the children ample time to develop their musical dialogues.

Ask some of the pairs of children to perform their musical dialogues for the rest of the class.

## Stage 3 - composing musical dialogues that end unexpectedly

*(An activity to do in pairs)*

For this activity, the children continue working with their stage 2 partners. Each pair composes an unexpected ending for its musical dialogue.

1.   Each pair of children experiments with ways to end its musical dialogue in an unexpected manner. There are many possible ways to end a musical dialogue. The final phrase might:

- contain unusual sounds;
- contain an unexpected pause;
- be louder or quieter than expected;
- contain an unusual rhythm.

2.   When the children have devised their endings, they may need to reconsider or slightly alter their dialogues.

3.   Ask some pairs of children to perform their completed musical dialogues. Afterwards, ask them to explain how they built up tension in the music and what they think made their endings unexpected.

**Musical skills and knowledge developed:**

- **Composing:** making up a musical dialogue; building up tension in music; making up phrases of different lengths
- **Pitch, duration, dynamics and tempo:** using these elements effectively to build up tension in music
- **Structure:** contrasting phrases; phrases of varied lengths; repetition

# Simple seasons

**S**wallows,
**P**rimroses
**R**eturn.
**It**'s
**N**ew,
**G**reen!

**S**kylarks
**U**p,
**M**eadows
**M**otley,
**E**lms
**R**egal.

......................................................................

**A**pples
**U**ntold,
**T**rees
**U**nruly;
**M**ists
**N**ow.

**W**aters
**I**cebound,
**N**aked
**T**rees;
**E**arth
**R**ests.

*Eric Finney*

# Simple seasons

In an acrostic, the first letter of each line when read vertically spells the subject of the poem.

The lines of 'Simple seasons' are each made up of one word. However, lines in acrostics usually consist of more than one word.

In the musical development activities that follow, the children divide into groups to make up music to reflect the mood of each season. The children then use their individual contributions to their pieces of music to make other pieces of music.

## Stage 1 · introducing acrostics

*(Whole class and small group activities)*

For this stage, the children learn about acrostics and write their own.

1.    Read 'Simple seasons' to the whole class. Ask the children about their responses to it.

2.    Read each acrostic slowly. Ask the children to write down the first letter of each word as you say it. Can the children spot the link between the poems and the words spelt out by the first letters?

3.    Divide the children into four groups. Allocate a season to each group. Each group thinks of words it associates with its season, then writes its own acrostic.

(In groups where there are six children, each child can contribute one line to the poem.)

4.    Ask some groups to read their acrostics to the rest of the class.

## Stage 2 · making up music for a season

*(A small group activity)*

The children remain in their groups from stage 1 to make up a piece of music capturing the mood and atmosphere of a season.

Have available a selection of tuned and untuned percussion instruments.

1.    Each group begins by considering the mood and atmosphere of its season. Do the children think of movement in their season? Summer heat is quite still, whereas there is movement in a blustery autumn day. Do the children think of their seasons as being happy, sad or both? A winter's day when the ground is covered with snow might seem sad and quiet - until children come out to play with snowballs.

2.    Each group then considers what qualities its piece of music should have in order to reflect the mood and atmosphere of its season. Guide the groups by asking some of the following questions:

- Will the piece of music have a melody?
- Will it have any pitched notes at all - such as chime bar notes or xylophone notes?
- Will it have short melodic patterns?
- Will the piece of music have a steady beat?
- Will there be long sounds, short sounds or both?
- Will the piece of music be loud, quiet, or both?
- Will it get louder, quieter, or both? If so, when will it get louder or quieter?
- How fast or slow will the piece of music be?
- Should it get faster, slower, or both? If so, when should it get faster or slower?

- Will everyone play at once?
- Will there be an agreed order in which the children take turns to play?
- What instruments will the group use?
- Will they use body percussion sounds and vocal sounds?
- How will the sounds be put together to make a piece of music?
- How will the piece of music end?

3.  The children experiment with sounds that might be appropriate for their pieces of music. They choose the sounds they like, refine them and organise them into pieces of music.

4.  When the groups are ready, they perform their compositions to the rest of the class.

5.  Ask the groups about the sounds they used in their pieces of music. In what ways do the children feel the sounds reflect the mood and atmosphere of the season on which the music is based?

## Stage 3 - developing music to represent all the seasons

*(A small group activity)*

In an acrostic, a word is made out of the first letters of several words. In this activity, new pieces of music are made out of parts of other pieces of music.

The children form new groups for this activity. Each child needs to remember his or her contribution to the stage 2 composition.

1.  Organise the children into their new groups. Each new group should have at least one child who was in a 'spring' group in stage 2, one who was in a 'summer' group, one from an 'autumn' group and one from a 'winter' group.

2.  Ask the groups to listen carefully as each of their members plays their contribution to the stage 2 piece of music. These are fragments or parts of the stage 2 compositions.

3.  The members of each new group now find ways of organising and combining the sounds they played in their stage 2 pieces of music to make one new piece of music. The new piece of music that emerges could be entitled 'Seasons'.

4.  Each group performs its new 'Seasons' piece of music for the rest of the class.

**Musical skills and knowledge developed:**
- **Composing:** making up music to reflect a mood or atmosphere; re-using sounds
- **Pitch, duration, dynamics, tempo, timbre, texture and structure:** using the elements effectively to create an intended mood or atmosphere

# I'm a parrot

I am a parrot
I live in a cage
I'm nearly always
in a vex-up rage

I used to fly
all light and free
in the luscious green
forest canopy

I am a parrot
I live in a cage
I'm nearly always
in a vex-up rage

I miss the wind
against my wing
I miss the nut
and the fruit picking

I am a parrot
I live in a cage
I'm nearly always
in a vex-up rage

I squawk I talk
I curse I swear
I repeat the things
I shouldn't hear

So don't come near me
or put out your hand
because I'll pick you
if I can
pickyou
pickyou
if I can

I want to be Free
Can't You Understand

*Grace Nichols*

# I'm a parrot

The stanzas of 'I'm a parrot' describe how the parrot once had freedom, how he misses that freedom and the anger he now feels. The refrain which recurs throughout the poem summarises the thoughts described in the stanzas.

In the musical development activities, the children make up pieces of music reflecting the moods of the stanzas of the poem.

## Stage 1 · introducing the poem

*(A whole class activity)*

You will need an enlarged photocopy of each of the pictures shown below, stuck on to card. Each is associated with a line of the refrain. Also make one photocopy showing all three pictures together.

1.  Read the poem to the children and discuss their reactions to it.

2.  Show the three pictures to the children. Explain that when you hold up a picture, the children chant the poem words associated with it. When you hold up the card showing all three pictures, the children chant the refrain.

3.  Each of the thoughts expressed in the refrain can be linked with a stanza. The first line of the refrain can be linked with the first stanza, the second line with the second stanza and the third and fourth lines with the third stanza. This is illustrated on the opposite page.

Perform the poem with the children joining in or interjecting with lines from the refrain. Hold up the card with all three pictures when the children can join in with the refrain. For the stanzas, hold up the appropriate card shown opposite so that the children can interject with a line linked with a stanza of the poem.

**I'm a parrot**

**I live in a cage**

**I'm nearly always
in a vex-up rage**

*I'm a parrot*
**I used to fly
all light and free
in the luscious green
forest canopy**

*I live in a cage*
**I miss the wind
against my wing
I miss the nut
and the fruit picking**

*I'm nearly always
in a vex-up rage*
**I squawk I talk
I curse I swear
I repeat the things
I shouldn't hear**

When you read the final stanza to the children,
show the cards in the following order:

*I'm a parrot*
**So don't come near me**

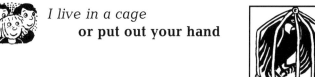

*I live in a cage*
**or put out your hand**

*I'm nearly always
in a vex-up rage*
**because I'll pick you
if I can**

In the composing activities that follow, the children
will focus on the first three stanzas. As in stage 1,
the 'I'm a parrot' picture will become associated
with the first stanza, the 'I live in a cage' picture
with the second stanza and the 'I'm nearly always
in a vex-up rage' picture with the third stanza.

## Stage 2 - preparing to make music reflecting the mood of a stanza

*(A small group activity)*

In this activity, the children choose a stanza and
explore its mood and atmosphere.

You will need photocopies of the pictures and a
selection of tuned and untuned percussion
instruments.

1.   Read out the three stanzas, holding up the
associated pictures. Then divide the children into
either six or nine groups.

Allocate a stanza to each group. If there are six
groups, choose two groups for each stanza; if there
are nine groups, choose three groups for each
stanza. Give each group a photocopy of the
picture associated with its stanza.

2.   Read the stanzas again so that each group can
carefully consider the mood and atmosphere of the
words. Ask each group whether the parrot in its
chosen stanza is miserable, happy, angry, furious,
lonely or bored. Did the parrot once have a better
life?

3.   Each group thinks about what qualities its
music should have in order to reflect the mood and
atmosphere of its stanza.

Here are some questions you can ask the children to help them make up their music.

Will the music sound most appropriate with:

- loud or quiet sounds?
- phrases or sections that get louder or quieter?
- fast or slow sounds?
- a fast or slow beat, or no beat at all?
- instrumental, body percussion or vocal sounds, or a combination of all three?

Each group should also consider:

- how to organise its music - should everyone perform at once, or should they start one at a time?
- whether to play repeated patterns or random sounds - could there be sections of both in the music?
- how the piece of music should begin and end.

4.    The groups explore sounds and experiment with musical ideas for their pieces of music.  Each group organises its sounds into a piece of music reflecting the mood and atmosphere of the chosen stanza.

5.    Each group shows its picture to indicate its stanza and performs the piece of music it composed for the rest of the class.

## Stage 3 - grouping together contrasting pieces of music

*(A whole class activity)*

In this activity, the groups experiment with joining three pieces of music together to make a longer piece capturing the different moods of the three stanzas from 'I'm a parrot'.

1.    Choose three groups, one for each stanza, to perform their pieces one after another to make a longer piece of music.  Order the three groups according to the order of their stanzas.

The children who are not performing listen.  They then discuss what they liked and didn't like about how the three pieces sounded together.

Ask the children what they thought of:
- the contrasts between the sections of music;
- the overall effect.

2.    Repeat the process of choosing a combination of three groups, one for each stanza, to perform together.  Follow it each time with a class discussion about how the pieces sound together. If you wish, the children may reach conclusions about which combinations of pieces they liked most.

**Musical skills and knowledge developed:**

- **Composing:** making up music that reflects feelings, mood and atmosphere; listening to, experimenting with and choosing sections of music that sound satisfactory together
- **Pitch, duration, dynamics, tempo, timbre and texture:** using the elements effectively to create a mood or atmosphere in music
- **Structure:** exploring contrast in different sections of music

# Acknowledgements

The following have kindly granted their permission for the reprinting of copyright material:

Neil Adams for **The song the train sang** © Neil Adams

John Agard c/o Caroline Sheldon Literary Agency for **Don't call alligator long-mouth till you cross river** by John Agard from *Say it again, Granny!* © 1986 John Agard, published by The Bodley Head. Reproduced by kind permission of John Agard.

Cambridge University Press for **The woodland haiku** by Wes Magee from *Morning Break and Other Poems.* © 1989 Cambridge University Press.

Chatto & Windus, part of Random House UK Limited, for **Mama Dot** by Fred D'Aguiar published by Chatto & Windus. Reprinted by permission.

Mary D Chauhan for **The swing (Moods of life)** © 1990 Mary D Chauhan.

Curtis Brown Ltd for **I'm a parrot** by Grace Nichols from *Come on into my Tropical Garden* published by A & C Black. © 1988 Grace Nichols. Reproduced by permission of Curtis Brown Ltd.

Farrar, Straus & Giroux, LLC for **The toaster** from *Laughing Time, Collected Nonsense* by William Jay Smith. © 1990 William Jay Smith. Reprinted by permission of Farrar Straus & Giroux, LLC.

Eric Finney for **Haiku** and **Simple seasons** © Eric Finney.

Fleetway Editions for **I'm a hip hoppy kid** by Kirtiss Horswell from *Verse Universe.* Reproduced by permission of Fleetway Editions.

David Higham Associates for **Cats** by Eleanor Farjeon from *The Childrens Bells* published by Oxford University Press © 1957. Reprinted by permission of David Higham Associates.

Little, Brown & Company for **Haiku** by David McCord from *One at a Time* by David McCord. © 1979 David McCord. Reprinted by permission of Little, Brown & Company.

Peters Fraser & Dunlop for **The leader** by Roger McGough from *Sky in the Pie* published by Viking Kestral, Penguin Books. © 1983 Roger McGough. Reprinted by permission of PFD on behalf of Roger McGough.

Jane Whittle for **The last exam** © Jane Whittle.

Every effort has been made to trace and acknowledge the copyright owners. If any right has been omitted, the publishers offer their apologies and will rectify this in subsequent editions following notification.

The authors and publisher would also like to thank the following people who have generously assisted in the preparation of this book: the staff and children of Richard Alibon Junior School, Barking; Thamesview Junior School, Barking; William Bellamy Junior School, Barking; Ray Mason of Music Education Supplies; Judith Palmer; Sheena Roberts; Jane Sebba; John Stephens, Head of Music Education and Development at Trinity College of Music.

## Index of poem titles

## Glossary of poetry terms

**Acrostic:** a poem in which the first letters of each line form a word or phrase.

**Haiku:** a traditional form of Japanese poetry. A haiku is made up of three lines: the first and last lines each contain five syllables and the middle line contains seven.

**Metaphor:** a form of expression in which something is described as something else.

**Refrain:** a group of lines in a poem forming a distinct section that is repeated in the poem between stanzas.

**Stanza:** a group of lines in a poem forming a distinct section.

**Villanelle:** a mediaeval poetry form containing six three line stanzas and a final four line stanza. Particular lines are repeated according to a fixed pattern.

## Glossary of musical terms

**Body percussion sounds:** see page 6.

**Duration:** *long and short sounds.* The length of a sound, note or silence.

**Dynamics:** *loud and quiet sounds.* The volume of a sound or section of music.

**Improvisation:** the process of creating music instantaneously; a piece of music made up as it is performed. Improvisations are not written down.

**Melody:** another word for a tune - an agreeable sequence of single notes.

**Notation:** the writing down of music in any form.

**Ostinato:** a pattern of sounds or notes that are repeated over and over again throughout a section or piece of music.

**Pace:** see tempo.

**Percussion - tuned and untuned:** see page 6.

**Phrase:** a short section or unit of a melody. Singers might breathe at the end of a phrase.

**Pitch:** sounds that can be described as high or low.

**Rhythms and rhythm patterns:** groupings of long sounds, short sounds and silences.

**Solo:** one person performing alone.

**Steady beat:** a regular pulse (sometimes heard but usually felt), marking equal measures of time. Marching soldiers and ticking clocks make the sound of a steady beat.

**Structure:** *sections, beginnings, endings, repetition, contrast.* How pieces of music are constructed.

**Tempo:** *fast and slow.* The speed of the beat in a piece of music.

**Texture:** the effect of a combination of sounds.

**Timbre:** sound quality; e.g. smooth, piercing, fuzzy...

**Vocal sounds:** see page 6.